Give your child a head start with
PICTURE READERS

Dear Parent,

Now children as young as preschool age can have the fun and satisfaction of reading a book all on their own.

In every Picture Reader, there are simple words, rebus pictures, and 24 flash cards to cut out and keep. (There is a flash card for every rebus picture plus extra cards for reading practice.) After children listen to each story a couple of times, they will be ready to try it all by themselves.

Collect all the titles in our Picture Reader series. Once children have mastered these books, they can move on to Levels 1, 2, and 3 in our All Aboard Reading series.

ISBN 0-448-41146-6 A B C D E F G H I J

A PICTURE READER

MONSTER
and
Muffin

By Joanna Cole
Illustrated by Karen Lee Schmidt

Grosset & Dunlap • New York

Monster was a

big brown .

He had a big blue .

He had a big red MONSTER.

He had a big white .

Monster had everything.

But he did not have a pal.

There was a

around his 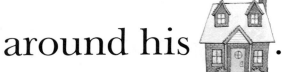.

No one came in.

They were scared

of the big .

A  named Muffin

lived in the next .

He was a small .

He was smaller than

Monster's big red  !

Muffin did not have

any pals.

He was scared

of everything.

And he barked a lot.

Yip! Yip!

Muffin barked at a .

Yip! Yip!

Muffin barked at a .

Yip! Yip!

He barked

at the new

down the block.

The mother

did not like that.

She tried to hit

Muffin on his 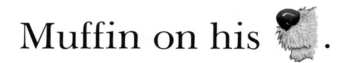.

Muffin ran away.

The

ran after Muffin.

They ran

past many

and under a 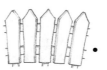.

It was Monster's 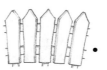.

Muffin stopped now.

He did not see

the big .

But the  saw him.

YOW!

She ran away.

"Wow!" said Muffin.

"I scared the away!"

Muffin saw

a big white .

Muffin saw

a big blue .

Then he saw

a big brown  —

a <u>very</u> big brown .

The big  gave

the little

a nice big kiss

on his 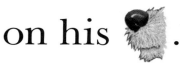 .

Muffin did not bark.

And he did not

run away.

And do you know what?

Now that great big

and that very small

are best pals.

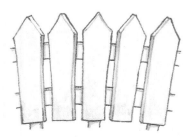

bed	dog
bone	bowl
house	fence

bunny	bird
cat	kitten
bow	nose

book	shirt
mouse	peas
sun	flower

grapes	ball
kite	train
cake	trees